Oh, My! Ginny

Waiting for Snow

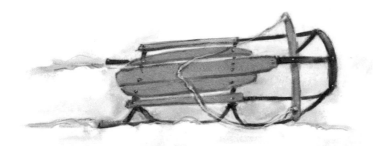

by Gina Shaw
Illustrated by Patrice Barton

Scholastic Inc.
New York Toronto London Auckland
Sydney Mexico City New Delhi Hong Kong

In memory of my dad, Tony,
and to my kids—Matt, Pam, Matt,
and Brian, who inspire me always.—G.S.

To Mac, John, and Shane—P.B.

ISBN 978-0-545-24385-8

Text copyright © 2010 by Gina Shaw
Illustrations copyright © 2010 by Patrice Barton
All rights reserved. Published by Scholastic Inc.

SCHOLASTIC and associated logos are trademarks
and/or registered trademarks of Scholastic Inc. Lexile
is a registered trademark of MetaMetrics, Inc.

12 11 10 9 8 7 6 5 4 3 2 1   10 11 12 13 14 15/0

Printed in the U.S.A.   40
First printing, December 2010

Book design by Jennifer Rinaldi Windau

Chapter 1

It is cold today at recess.

I run over to Spike.

He is my best friend.

I tug on his coat.

"Guess what," I say.

"What?" Spike asks.

I jump up and down.

I twirl around and around.

"My mom and I found
Grandpa Tony's old sled
in the attic last night. I'm
going to try it out when the
snow comes."

"Wow!" Spike says. "Can I ride
it, too?"

"Sure!" I say. "We'll go down hills together. It will be fun. But the sled's so old. I just hope it works."

"Thanks!" says Spike. "Don't worry. The sled will work."

Now, we both can't wait for it to snow.

Yayyy for us!

Chapter 2

The school bell rings.

Everyone lines up and

goes inside the building.

Spike and I are in Class 1-11.

I sit in the first row next

to the coat closet.

We all hang up our jackets.

We do our jobs.

I water the plants.

Spike feeds Rocky, our class bird.

Then, we sit down in our seats.

"Ginny," Ms. Hurley says, "I have a surprise for you."

"A surprise for me!" I shout. "What is it? What is it?"

I jump out of my seat.

I raise my arms high in the air.

I cheer.

Everyone stares at me.

"Ginny, please sit down," Ms. Hurley
says.

Ms. Hurley is very polite.

She always says "Please" and

"Thank you."

But I know Ms. Hurley is serious.

So, I sit down right away.

"Boys and girls," Ms. Hurley says,
"remember when we chose
pen pals from Alaska to write to
last month?"

"Yes," everyone says.

PEN PALS

ETHAN
SIERRA
MADISON
JACOB
EMILY
GRACE
WILLIAM
MICHAEL
LILY
LOGAN
AVA

"Well, Ginny's new pen pal

has written back to her,"

Ms. Hurley says.

Everyone in the class looks at me.

I am the first one to get a letter.

"Wow!" I say.

Spike gives me a great, big smile.

He is happy for me.

Spike is always happy for me.

"Here's your letter," Ms. Hurley

says. "Would you like to read it

to the class?"

"Yes, yes, yes!" I say.

Ms. Hurley hands me the letter.

I can't wait to open it.

I'm so excited!

Dear Ginny,

You are so funny.
I'm glad you're my pen pal.
Here are my answers to
your questions.
My full name is
Sierra Aubrey Cly.
You're right! Cly does
rhyme with Fry.
I live in Nome, Alaska.
No, I don't have a best
friend named Spike.
No, I don't have a pet bird.
No, I do have a dog named
Wink.

Yes, we get lots and lots
of snow here.
I just got a new sled.
It goes very fast down
big hills.
Sometimes, Wink pulls my sled.
What do you do in the snow?

Write soon.
Sierra

"Ooh, I like Sierra," I tell my class.

"And look, she sent two pictures of

Wink pulling her new sled."

"How nice!" Ms. Hurley says.

I look at the kids in my class.

"I hope it snows soon," I say.

"I found my Grandpa Tony's
old sled in the attic last night.
It doesn't look like Sierra's new sled.
But now, Spike and I can't wait to go
sledding. I just hope my sled will work."

"I want to go sledding,"

says Spike.

"Me, too," says Bond.

"Me, three," says Alice.

But there isn't any snow yet.

So, we'll all have to wait.

Too bad for us!

Chapter 3

"Class," Ms. Hurley says, "we're going to make a Welcome Winter snow scene for our classroom. We will put it on the back shelf."

"Yayyy!" everyone shouts.

"Here's what you will do," Ms. Hurley says.

"Ginny, you will make the snow from soap flakes, water, and glue," Ms. Hurley says. "Spike, you will paint the snow. Dustin, you will make the snowmen. Jody, you will add the hills. Everyone else will cut out paper snowflakes to hang around the the room. Now, please go to your worktables and begin."

"Yayyy!" everyone shouts again.

But not me.

I don't like mixing soap flakes, water,

and glue together.

It makes my hands feel **YUCKY!**

Spike walks over to me.

He is unhappy, too.

"I don't want to paint the snow,"

he says. "I can only paint it white.

That's **BOR-ING!**"

We sit down at our worktable.

We put our heads in our hands.

Then we both look up at each other.

We smile.

We giggle.

We laugh out loud.

"Let's switch jobs!" we say together.

"But, let's ask Ms. Hurley first,"

Spike says.

I agree.

Ms. Hurley says yes.

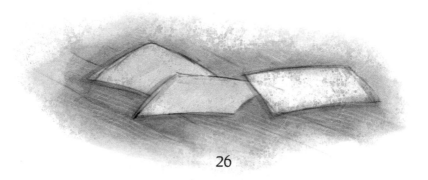

So, Spike makes the snow.

He likes the **YUCKY** feeling of

mixing the soap flakes, water,

and glue together.

I take out winter white, light gray,

and sky blue paint.

I swirl them together and paint

the snow.

Everyone likes my colors.

My snow is not **BOR-ING!**

When I am finished painting,

I walk to the window.

I look outside.

When will it snow? I wonder.

I can't wait too much longer.

But I will have to.

Too bad for me!

Chapter 4

One week goes by.

Monday is show-and-tell.

My mom carries Grandpa

Tony's sled to school.

She stays to watch me tell

the class about my grandpa's

sled.

"This is my Grandpa Tony's sled,"

I say. "It is made of wood. It is old.

My mom and I found it in the attic."

I sit down.

I am still worried.

I hope my grandpa's sled

will work.

But, I'm not so sure.

And if we don't get any snow, I

will never know.

"Everyone, stand up," Ms. Hurley

says. "Let's shake out our hands

and feet."

We all get out of our seats and

stand next to our desks.

Spike raises his hand high.

Ms. Hurley calls on him.

"Can we sing our snowflake song
for Ginny's mom?" he asks.
Spike always knows how to cheer
me up.
"What a good idea, Spike!" Ms. Hurley
says. "Okay, class—1, 2, 3."

I'm a little snowflake.

You can see . . .

no other snowflake

looks like me!

Please pick me up

after I fall.

Then roll me into

a big snowball.

My mom claps and thanks

us all for our song.

"You were great!" she says.

Yayyy for us!

Chapter 5

My mom leaves our room.

She takes my grandpa's sled

with her.

I think about the snow again.

Then, I think about Sierra.

During free time, I write to her.

snow →

Dear Sierra,
I like your new sled.
Thank you for sending me a
picture of it.
I showed it to my class.
You are lucky to have
so much snow.
We don't have any snow.
Zip! Zero! No snow!!!
I want to use my grandpa's
sled.
I want to see if it works.
Think of me when you go fast
down those big hills.
Write again soon.
Ginny

Suddenly, I hear Spike shouting

from across the room.

I look up.

He is at the window.

"It's snowing!" he yells.

I jump up.

So does everyone else.

Spike really does know how

to cheer me up.

"Please sit down," Ms. Hurley says.

"I will give each row a turn

to look at the snow."

Ms. Hurley calls the row
closest to the window first.
Then, she calls the fourth,
third, and second rows.
Now it is my row's turn.
The five of us stand up.

We go to the window and

look out.

Oh, no!

The snow has stopped.

Too bad for us!

Chapter 6

I feel sad.

We all go back to our seats.

"I'm sorry, boys and girls,"

Ms. Hurley says. "I know how

much you want it to snow.

I have an idea. Let's have a

Welcome Winter party."

Ms. Hurley tells us to get our coats.

We are going home right

after our party.

We walk down to the lunchroom.

Ms. Hurley gives us each a cup

of cocoa.

She gives us little snow white

marshmallows, too.

I start to feel better.

Soon, it's time to go home.

We head to the school yard.

Wow!

It snowed while we were

having our party.

There is snow everywhere!

I see my mom.

She has Grandpa Tony's sled

with her.

She pulls me and Spike

home on it.

Along the way, we stop at a

big hill.

Whee! We go down the hill

on Grandpa's sled!

Yayyy for us!

Dear Sierra,
Guess what?
It finally snowed here.
And our school is closed
for a snow day!
Spike and I have been
riding Grandpa Tony's
sled for hours.
It works!
Write soon.

Ginny